ƎCBC

A PERSONAL PROMISE FOR

Jordan Bischoff

"You can be sure that I will be with you always."

—JESUS (MATTHEW 28:20)

Adapted from *The Easter Promise* video © 1996 by Christian Broadcasting Network.
Published in Nashville, Tennessee, by Tommy Nelson™, a division of Thomas Nelson, Inc.

Scripture quotation is from *The International Children's Bible, New Century Version,*
copyright © 1986, 1988 by Word Publishing. Used by permission.

Library of Congress Cataloging-in-Publication Data

Cochran, Brian.
    The Easter promise /original story by Brian Cochran; text adaptation by Lila Empson;
art direction by Angela Costello & Lindy Powell.
        p. cm.
    Summary: Three children follow the events that lead Jesus from his joyous entry into Jerusalem
to his betrayal, death, and resurrection.
    ISBN 0-8499-5827-X
    1. Jesus Christ—Passion—Juvenile fiction. 2. Jesus Christ—Resurrection—Juvenile
fiction. [1. Jesus Christ—Passion—Fiction. 2. Jesus Christ—Resurrection—Fiction. 3.
Easter—Fiction.]   I. Empson, Lila. II. Costello, Angela Ward. III. Powell, Linda. IV. Title.
PZ7.C6393Eas   1998
[E]—dc21   97-47682
                                                                                                          CIP
                                                                                                          AC

Printed in the United States of America

98 99 00 01 02 LBM 9 8 7 6 5 4 3 2 1

THE EASTER PROMISE

Original story by Brian Cochran
Text adaptation by Lila Empson
Art direction by Angela Costello & Lindy Powell

Tommy
NELSON

Thomas Nelson, Inc.
Nashville

Lazarus was sick. Mary and Martha knew that
Jesus could make him well—if he would only get there
in time.

But Lazarus died. Jesus was too late to help him.
Or was he?

Jesus could do things that no one else could do.

He brought Lazarus back to life.

Lazarus's sisters were not the only ones who believed in Jesus. Many people wanted to follow Jesus.

That made the Pharisees mad. They didn't like Jesus. They wanted to stop him—no matter what.

Jerem and Elizabeth did not know anything about Jesus or the Pharisees. They liked to climb high in their favorite tree, watch people go by, and dream about what they would be when they grew up. One day they heard Roman guards marching by with a prisoner.

"Soldiers!" Jerem shouted excitedly.

Elizabeth felt sorry for the prisoner.

But Jerem liked the soldiers' shiny armor and swords. He wanted to be a soldier some day.

"Elizabeth, Jerem," their mother called.

Elizabeth and Jerem slid down. Cousin Samuel and Uncle Jacob had come to visit.

Uncle Jacob was excited. "A king is coming to Jerusalem, and he will be in need of some very special soldiers."

"When is he coming?" Jerem wanted to know.

"Tomorrow."

"Samuel, come on!" cried Jerem. "We do not have much time to make my armor for the king."

The next day was the Passover holiday.

Elizabeth and Samuel waited for Jerem. What was taking him so long?

Jerem was putting on soldier clothes.

He would guard the mighty king that Uncle Jacob had told him about.

They heard the noise of an oncoming crowd and rushed up in their favorite tree for a better look.

The crowd shouted, "The king of kings has arrived!"

"Where is he?" asked Jerem. "Where are his chariots and soldiers?"

Then Jerem saw Jesus. He did not look like a king at all.
He looked like a man riding a donkey.

Jerem was disappointed.

The soldiers laughed at Jesus—and they laughed at
Jerem too.

Samuel tried to explain. "Jesus is the king of all kings."
But Jerem was mad. "I am taking this stupid armor off."
Then Jerem slipped and fell. He hit the ground hard.
"Jerem!" Elizabeth cried.

Jerem lay on the ground. Was he dead?

Jesus knelt beside Jerem and touched him. "Get up, child. You are better now."

And he was!

"Leave me alone. I do not need your help," Jerem yelled at Jesus.

"Stop laughing at me," he yelled at the soldiers.

"Jesus is no king," he yelled at the crowd.

Jerem was confused and upset.

The Pharisees were watching Jerem. Later, they offered him a job.

The Pharisees tricked Jerem into doing a mean thing.

Jesus was chasing out thieves, but Jerem told everyone that Jesus was tearing up the temple.

The Pharisees were happy. They rewarded Jerem with a shiny gold coin for what he did!

Jerem walked away and climbed a tree.

He could see and hear the Pharisees and Jesus. Jesus gave very smart answers to very hard questions.

Uncle Jacob searched for Jerem and found him in a tree. "Always be careful whom you trust," he warned.

That night Jerem had a scary dream. He woke up and ran outside. Elizabeth and Samuel followed him.

"What if we are wrong about Jesus?" Jerem asked the Pharisees.

But the Pharisees were too busy to bother with them. They were talking to another man who had a plan to trap Jesus.

"Why do the Pharisees hate Jesus?" Jerem asked.

"Maybe they are afraid of him," said Elizabeth.

"Because maybe he is who he says he is," said Samuel.

"Come on. We have to find Jesus and warn him," Jerem said.

Samuel, Elizabeth, and Jerem searched everywhere.

When they found Jesus he was eating the Passover meal with his friends, who were his disciples.

But one of Jesus' friends—Judas—looked familiar. He was the stranger who had been talking with the Pharisees!

Jesus did not need to be warned. He knew Judas would betray him.

"Go," Jesus said to Judas. "Do what you must." And Judas left.

Later, Jesus prayed in the garden while his friends slept.

Soldiers came to the garden with Judas, and he walked boldly up to Jesus. Judas kissed Jesus on the cheek. That was the signal.

Then Jesus was taken to the Pharisee leaders. "Are you the Son of God?"

"I am," Jesus said truthfully.

"Take him to Pilate!"

Pilate could free one prisoner—either Jesus, who was innocent of any crime, or a guilty man named Barabbas. Pilate was afraid to choose, so he let the people decide.

"We choose Barabbas," the people yelled.

The soldiers put a crown of thorns on Jesus and beat him. They laughed at Jesus for thinking he was God's son.

Then the soldiers hanged Jesus on a cross between two thieves.

"Father, forgive them," Jesus prayed. "Into your hands I commit my spirit."

The wind blew. The ground quaked. The earth cried.

Jesus was dead.

The children were very sad.

Jesus' followers wrapped his body in cloth and put his body in a tomb.

His followers closed the entrance with a gigantic stone so no one would disturb Jesus' body.

On the third day, the three children sat in a tree thinking about what had happened.

"Angels, angels!" A soldier bounded past.

Angels?

The three children hurried to the tomb. The big stone had been rolled away!

The children followed some women inside.

Jesus was gone.

"I know you are looking for Jesus, but he is not here," an angel said. "Jesus is risen from the dead."

They ran through the streets. They knocked on doors.
They shouted from the rooftops.

"It is time to celebrate. Jesus has risen from the grave.
He is alive!"

Later, Jesus appeared to believers and said, "Preach the Good News to everyone. Those who believe and are baptized will be saved. And be sure of this. I will be with you always!"

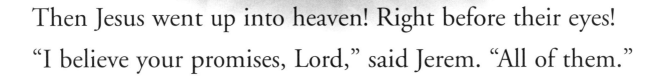

Then Jesus went up into heaven! Right before their eyes!
"I believe your promises, Lord," said Jerem. "All of them."